T0147923

Stories To Celebrate Life

Stories To Celebrate Life

Stories for the young and young at heart…

ENG FOO TIAM

PARTRIDGE

A Penguin Random House Company

| ISBN: | Softcover | 978-1-4828-2886-3 |
| | eBook | 978-1-4828-2887-0 |

To order additional copies of this book, contact
Toll Free 800 101 2657 (Singapore)
Toll Free 1 800 81 7340 (Malaysia)
orders.singapore@partridgepublishing.com

www.partridgepublishing.com/singapore

Contents

To my beloved students

Thank you for the journey through life

1

The Seventh Step

Something weird happened to Lay See when she was playing hopscotch with some of her girlfriends. When it was her turn to play, Lay See skipped seven steps and when she turned round, her friends were nowhere in sight! Instead, standing before her very eyes were three of the fattest hens she had ever seen!

"Oh dear," The first hen clucked, "Don't just stand there, Lay See!"

"We are your friends!" The second hen said, "I suppose you can see very well the change in us!"

The third hen then explained, "A temperamental magician passed by when your back was turned. We were giggling among ourselves and he had thought that we were laughing at him. In a fit of anger, he had cast a spell on us, turning us all into these big, fat hens!"

"Help us regain our original forms, Lay See," The first hen urged, "We are hens now and hens can't do much compared to a human being." The second hen explained, "People don't listen to hens!"

"Run down the silver road ahead quickly and if we are lucky, you can still catch up with the magician," The third hen instructed. "The magician may be temperamental but he is still kind and will listen to reasons. If you explain to him what actually happened, he may yet turn us back into human beings."

"Run, Lay See, run!" The three hens then clucked simultaneously, creating such a din. "Our fate is in your hand!"

Lay See ran as fast as her feet could carry her. When she came to a junction however, she had to stop to ponder over which road to take.

"Where are you heading to, child?" a green bird perched on a branch of a banyan tree asked when it saw Lay See.

"I am trying to catch up with a magician," Lay See replied. "And kind sir, if you have in any way seen which road he took; do tell me so since my friends' very fate depend very much on it."

Lay See went on to explain what had happened and the bird suddenly turned grave.

Now, the bird was not as kind as you'd have thought. It was a very cunning creature and had worn a serious countenance merely because it was seriously contemplating on tricking Lay See into becoming a maid in its house.

"Take the road on your right!" The bird said, "The magician's house is a green cottage at the end of the road."

Lay See thanked the bird and went on her way. When she reached the end of the road, she knocked on the door of the green cottage and was surprised to find it opened by the very same green bird she had met earlier.

"Is the magician in?" Lay See asked, trying not to look surprised.

"I am the magician," the bird claimed. The cunning bird had earlier directed Lay See to its own house and had unknown to her, flown quickly home to wait on her.

"My magic has informed me why you are here," the bird then lied and pretended to be very angry. "If you ever want me to help your rude friends, then you will have to work hard in keeping my house clean for one whole year!" It said.

Lay See who had not laid her eyes on the magician before had thought that he had transformed himself into a bird. She was therefore easily led into believing the imposter.

"I…I …I'm just here to explain and apologize on behalf of my friends," Lay See stammered.

"I know, I know," the bird said.

Meanwhile, the magician who was looking into his crystal ball saw all that had happened. He was so angry with the bird for trying to trick a young innocent girl that he instantly turned it into an ugly toad!

As for Lay See's friends, the magician was very apologetic.

When Lay See later resumed her game of hopscotch, she just had to hop seven steps and when she turned round, there before her very eyes were again her three lovely friends. She felt so much relieved since for a moment ago, at the prospect of losing her friends, she had felt so much emptiness.

2

The Boy, The Bird and The Egg

Chee Siong, the boy who was not yet eight, was full of spirits when he woke up one Sunday morning. He put on his favourite yellow T-shirt and his new Bermuda shorts and in no time at all, was at the kitchen table, enjoying the piping hot porridge that his mother had dished out and a cup or two of her steaming black coffee.

Chee Siong was as cheery as the morning sun. Gaily, he poured into the aquarium in the living room, some greenish fish pellets which the black angelfish greedily gobbled up.

"Don't be greedy, my dear angels!" Chee Siong chirped before skipping out into the garden.

Outside, the morning sun welcomed Chee Siong with a gentle slap on his cheeks.

Oh! How rosy Chee Siong's cheeks were! How happy and pleased he was especially when he found an empty bird nest in a rose bush.

"There should be an egg in the nest!" Chee Siong said.

He skipped quickly into the kitchen and when his mother was not looking, pinched a little milky white egg with brown spots from a blue Tupperware on the kitchen table.

The nest in the rose bush would now have an egg!

Chee Siong's eyes gleamed with joy and his little hands almost trembled when he placed the egg in the nest.

The little egg seemed tailored-made for the nest! How snug and cosy it looked as it laid motionless there!

Meanwhile, the bird, a beautiful little yellow creature, was perching on the cherry tree. It had been singing all morning and was getting very thirsty. It pecked at an over-ripe cherry to drink its juice and when it had enough of its fill, its eyes suddenly started to grow heavy with drowsiness.

"Oh, I think I need a rest!" The bird chirped. " Morning seems like a great time for a nap and a bird needs its rest too!"

The little yellow bird spotted the nest in the rose bush.

"Ah! There is an abandoned nest there!" The little bird chirped gaily and thought, "I bet the owner would not mind at all if I take a short nap there."

It flew swiftly to nestle in the nest.

What a comfortable nest that turned out to be! The downy feathers, which lined the inside of the nest, were so soft and there was something deliciously hard underneath!

"Oh! I could sit here for days!" The little yellow bird then chirped before dozing off.

And it must be days that it sat there in the nest, dozing!

The little yellow bird only woke up when it felt something moving underneath. It bent its head to look and was surprised indeed to see another brown bird staring up at it with wide, innocent eyes!

"Oh! It's a little quail! The little yellow bird exclaimed. "How silly of me to sit on a quail's egg," It said but felt happy nevertheless.

When Chee Siong skipped into the garden to check on the egg in the nest, he was surprised to find instead the little quail.

When he saw the little yellow bird nursed the little quail, his face started to beam. There are others who care too, it seems.

3

The Grape Escaped

A hawker, who was selling fruits in a bustling market, was so busy tending to his customers that he failed to notice that a grape that he was selling had detached itself from a bunch and made good its escape.

A fat woman carrying a big empty basket had earlier said to the hawker, "Can you please give me two kilos of grapes? I hope they are sweet. My children simply love sweet grapes."

"They are sweet, madam," the hawker said and his hands went instinctively for a bunch.

"Oh, oh… I've better be going," the grape had said just then. "I'm not going to end up as food for some brats!"

Jumping down from the basket it was in, the grape rolled down the road. It was very lucky indeed not to be squashed by the people plying the street.

Coming to a green meadow, the grape had jumped onto a big black rock to rest when suddenly, it felt the rock moving.

"Oh, oh…" The grape said. "There is an earthquake!"

It rolled down from the rock only to be confronted by a long, slender black head, which had poked out from the rock.

The grape had sat on a tortoise!

"Hullo," the tortoise greeted. "Are you a grape?" It asked.

"I am," the grape said proudly.

"Oh! It's a long time since I last tasted a grape!" The tortoise said and its mouth began to water. "Can I have a bite of you?" It asked.

"Oh, no, you can't!" The grape said and started to roll away quickly. It was a good thing that the tortoise was such a slow creature.

The grape rolled and rolled until it came to the edge of the forest.

There, it was surprised to meet an old wolf.

"Are you a wolf?" The grape asked curiously.

"Yes, I am," the wolf replied.

"I haven't heard of a wolf living in the forest in this part of the world," the grape said.

"Oh, I have escaped from the zoo and I have actually run a very great distance," the wolf explained and said, "Now, I am also very tired and thirsty and if you don't mind, I would like to eat you!"

"Oh! You silly old wolf!" The grape said. "Of course, I do mind!"

The wolf, nevertheless, tried to eat the grape. It snapped at it with its mouth but the grape managed to escape by jumping quickly into a very deep hole in the ground.

The wolf then tried to get at the grape by putting its paw into the hole but the hole was too deep.

After trying very hard for a couple of hours, the wolf simply gave up.

"Oh, maybe, I shouldn't eat you at all," the wolf said. "You are so dirty with all that dirt on your skin and for all I know, you may even be just a little brown pebble passing for a grape!"

"Oh, I am a grape all right!" The grape said crossly and shook off the dirt from its skin.

"Oh, you are just a little green grape!" The wolf then exclaimed. "For all I know, a green grape is really, very, very sour!"

Now the grape was getting really, really cross!

"The hawker had said that I was a very sweet grape! I still am!" It yelled and jumped out of the hole instantly to confront the wolf.

When the grape emerged from the hole, the wolf had immediately snapped at it with its mouth.

This time, the grape did not escape.

4

The Grasshopper And
The Caterpillar

The grasshopper lived in a very well tended garden where there was myriad of flowers all year round. Food was never scarce in this tropical paradise and the grasshopper would get to play every day if his heart so desired.

One day, the grasshopper invited his neighbour, the ant, out to play whereupon they came upon a little silvery ball on the leaf of a sunflower.

"What a beautiful ball this is!" The grasshopper chirped excitedly. "It's a pity that it sticks so firmly on the leaf's surface. Otherwise, we could take it home to play with."

Days later, when the two neighbours again came to play, the ball was nowhere to be seen. Instead, there was a big, fat green caterpillar that chomped away at the sunflower leaf.

"Hullo," the ant greeted politely. "You must be the new kid in the neighbourhood," he said. "I can't remember seeing you here before."

The caterpillar nodded his head silently as he continued to chip away on the sunflower leaf.

"You look very different from others," the grasshopper had then said rudely. "Your eyes are big and dare I say, bulge terribly that I would swear that you are by far, the ugliest creature I have ever met."

When the ant invited the caterpillar to play with them, the grasshopper was not at all pleased.

"I don't think that would be wise," He brushed away the idea. "Mr. Caterpillar does not look like he is fit enough to play. Being the glutton he is, you can see very well he is rather fat and would be either too clumsy or too slow in his movement. I bet he can't even walk fast enough to keep up with us."

Almost immediately, the caterpillar's eyes glazed all over.

The grasshopper and the ant failed to see the caterpillar anywhere on the sunflower leaf the next time they were there. They, however, managed to locate a little brown nut.

"What a strange nut this is!" The ant exclaimed excitedly. "I have never in my life seen a nut that attached itself to a leaf and this one lives!"

"Something inside is trying very hard to come out," the grasshopper added as excitedly. "It's a butterfly!"

And what a beautiful butterfly it was! Its dazzling, red, white and black wings immediately smote the grasshopper.

"Hi!" The grasshopper chirped gaily to greet the butterfly and was very prompt to offer his friendship.

"Would I be honoured indeed to meet a new friend!" He said.

"But I'm not as new a friend as you think I am!" The butterfly retorted. "I am the former Mr. Caterpillar that you so despised!"

"And to tell you the truth, your scalding remarks earlier had hurt me so much that for a while, I sealed myself off in a cocoon, never intending to see anyone again in my life!" The caterpillar confided before adding, "But I'll still be your friend yet Mr. Grasshopper, if you can answer this simple question: If before, as a caterpillar, you could not love me as just another being, can you now, possibly love me as a friend when in all my glory, I am basically still the same old caterpillar?"

When the grasshopper failed to reply, the butterfly flew off to gather nectar. There is much sweetness yet in life.

5

A Beauty And A Beast

A crown prince of a very big and prosperous country found it very hard to find a bride. When he was of marriageable age, his father tried to match him with several princesses from neighbouring countries but each of his attempts proved to be unsuccessful.

On one occasion, the prince heard from merchants who came to trade in his country of a certain Princess Fragrance. The merchants spoke of a very pretty princess, not yet eighteen, who had become the toast among princes the world over. The princess belonged to an equally big and powerful nation and though had received many offers for her hand in marriage, had rejected all such offers.

As it would have it, on reaching his destination, the prince was welcomed by the sight of a long line of people along the dusty road near the market place. A pleasant scent like fresh flowers wafted to his nose and he heard the sound of cymbals and drums as a procession came into view. Someone in the crowd whispered that Princess Fragrance was on her way to pray at the local temple and there she was, reclining comfortably on the beautifully carved palanquin carried by four very muscular guards!

Amidst the clouds of dust stirred up by the procession, the prince could see faintly the princess covering her face partially with a white feather fan. Momentarily, when the cloud of dust wafted, he would catch glimpses of her wide doe-like eyes whose long lashes were as dark as her long smooth silky hair. Dressed in a flowing white mink gown, her fair skin had also appeared whiter than the whitest polar bear and as she lay there on the palanquin, she looked very much like a prized Persian cat.

The prince followed the procession to the temple ground. There, when the princess alighted from her palanquin, he could see clearly for himself that the princess was what the merchants said she was. Having a very pretty figure and being very small in stature, she was as dainty as a newborn lamb. Princess Fragrance was indeed the prettiest and daintiest princess of them all! As she flitted like a butterfly with her maids across the temple garden, her laughter seemed to fill the air like the chirping of birds on a fine sunny morning.

On that fine sunny morning too, Princes Fragrance transformed suddenly like a chameleon. When one of her maids accidentally stepped on and dirtied her flowing white mink gown, her face had suddenly turned dark with fury. Her eyes started to bulge like those of a goldfish and as she raised her slender hands to hit the poor maid, the prince could see that she had nails like talons. She scratched at the maid's face like a cat and shrieked verbal abuses at her like a monkey. She was very angry that her expensive mink gown had been ruined and she decided then that she would return immediately to the palace.

Rushing down a flight of stairs to her waiting palanquin, the princess had looked like a furious tigress running after its prey. On her way, she had bumped into the prince and instead of apologizing, she had snarled at him like a mad dog. Close up, the prince could see that her teeth were as sharp as a wolf's and there were even blemishes on her face, quite unlike a toad's. Ah! Princess Fragrance was more a beast than a beauty.

The prince decided then to make for home. Riding his white stallion through the jungle, he had encountered far nicer beasts.

6

The Emperor's New Robe

You'd probably have heard of an emperor who had been conned by a bunch of cunning tailors because of the former's love for clothes but once, a long, long time ago before this emperor was ever conned, there was yet another as vain an emperor whose sheer love for clothes brought him uncalled for trouble. This emperor would buy new clothes in the thousands and getting tired of them very quickly, would discard them without as much as a second thought.

The emperor was also very fussy about his clothes. When he was turning forty, he planned a big celebration and had a hard time scouting for a new clothe to go with his new diamond-studded crown. Bazaars far and wide were combed, but there was no attire that suited him and the tailors who offered to help, failed to come up with a suitable design.

Just when the emperor thought that he was at his wit's end, ten foreign tailors from the west dropped by his palace to pay their tributes. The tailors were on their way to Japan to discuss a new dress for a Japanese princess. The emperor persuaded them to stay a little longer in his country and commissioned them to design a special suit, making them an offer that they could not refuse.

For ten days and ten nights, the ten foreign tailors toiled. Each came up with designs after designs but none seemed to please the emperor.

On the tenth day however, the ten tailors worked together and came up with a fabulous idea. The tailors proposed a high-collared flowing robe with a train so long that it would require a hundred train-bearers. And the train would have auspicious motifs of dragons and pearls, quadrupeds and flowers, all sewn with precious stones and gold thread to symbolize good fortune and success.

A hundred tailors were then engaged to do the sewing. For ten days and ten nights, the hundred tailors sewed. When at last, the last precious stone was stitched, the emperor was extremely pleased with the result that he rewarded the ten foreign tailors each with an extra ten gold ingots. The emperor had never in his entire life, laid his eyes on such beautiful and elaborate, yet exquisite attire ever!

During his fortieth birthday bash, ten male servants were required to just help the emperor put on his new robe. The emperor was indeed a sight to behold! A hundred little girls all dressed in white lacy frocks and wearing fresh flowers on their hair, became the train-bearers and the emperor practically glittered when he walked down the aisle to this throne. And he was proud to hear his subjects gasped in admiration all along the way!

"His Majesty is so handsome!" One starry-eyed girl in the crowd gasped aloud.

"His Majesty looked like a constellation of stars!" Another as starry-eyed bespectacled boy who was clutching a book on astronomy added.

"His Majesty walks so slowly and with such a majestic gait," an old man with grey hair said.

"His Majesty is very healthy too," a peasant who had not seen the emperor in person before, concluded, "His face is so pink with health!"

"But hey, wait a minute!" Someone else in the crowd then interrupted. "His face is not pink! It was pink before but it is changing its hue! His Majesty's face is turning blue!"

At this moment, the emperor just dropped to the ground. Alas, the emperor's new robe had proven to be too heavy for him. What had transpired was this: The sheer weight of the precious stones on the emperor's robe had taken its toll on the emperor. The emperor was so tired! He could not walk any faster and plodding along the long aisle to his throne, the old man had thought that the emperor had walked with a majestic gait. When the emperor's face turned red as a result of over-exertion, the peasant had interpreted that as his pink face of health. When the emperor was almost reaching his throne, the long, heavy train seemed to strangle him and as he ran out of air, his face turned blue.

For ten days and ten nights afterwards, the emperor had to recuperate in bed. You'd have thought that the emperor would get rid of his new robe after this like he did the others; but really, his new robe was very, very expensive. Emperors too, have second thoughts.

7

Three Foolish Men

A youngster eager to play a prank on three foolish men did so by inviting them to his birthday party which he said was held in the middle of the forest.

"Why do you hold your party in the forest?" One of the foolish men asked curiously. Foolish as he was, he was still smart enough to be aware that no one in his village had yet to hold a party there.

"Oh, I like it to be in the midst of nature," the youngster said.

When the second foolish man asked why the party was held in the afternoon and not at night like most other parties, the youngster merely said, "Oh, then, it would be too dark and I would have to buy lamps to light up the place. I couldn't possibly have afforded that!"

And all the while when the two curious foolish men posed their questions, the third foolish man would just stand there, grinning from ear to ear and nodding his head in agreement to each of the youngster's seemingly sensible replies.

On the day when the birthday party was supposed to take place, the poor three foolish men trudged in single file into the forest, each bearing as gifts; a red, orange and yellow parcel decorated by a huge green, blue and indigo ribbon respectively.

The three foolish men were all also specially dressed up in the same silk shirt and matching long pants. While the first foolish man wore polka dotted deep purple shirt and pants, his two foolish friends went for stripes and checks in a variety of bright gaudy colours. The three foolish men were indeed a sight to behold and boy, did they make heads turn! Some kids mistook them for part of a procession while adults were amused to see them so serious, trudging in a line with half-shut eyes and their nose high up in the air!

The poor three foolish men must have walked for miles and miles. Their clothes became drenched with sweat and when one started to pant, another started to complain of aching feet and the other, of thirst. All agreed to take a rest on the cool spot under a big, shady tree but had hardly sat down on a rock when the leaves behind them started to rustle.

The three foolish men turned their heads in unison and when confronted by a robust old man with a large forehead and snowy, white hair, their mouths dropped open one after another.

The strange old man walked slowly towards them with the aid of a crooked golden walking stick and had in his left hand, a very large queer-looking red fruit.

"You poor dear! You must be full of thirst!" The old man exclaimed and kindly offered, "Come, take this fruit. It will pep you up in no time!"

"Whatever this fruit is!" The first foolish man exclaimed the moment the strange old man left.

"It's far too big to be a cherry, isn't it?" The second foolish man said and added, "It must be a melon!"

"A melon has green skin, you silly; and is twice as big. It has to be an apple," the first foolish man said while the third foolish man nodded his head, grinning from ear to ear.

Just then, the leaves behind them rustled again and who would appear but the youngster, who while not really celebrating any birthday, was out to trick the foolish men of their gifts.

"Hey, what's that red fruit that you've got there?" He asked, his eyes gleaming.

"Oh, a page has given it to us to quench our thirst," the first foolish man replied.

"Now, you are being silly. It's a sage you meant," the second foolish man said.

"Actually, it's a strange old man who gave us this," the second foolish man then said and asked the youngster to help identify the fruit.

The youngster pretended to think hard.

"Mmmm…mmm... Maybe, I can tell if you allow me to take a bite of the fruit," He said and went on to take a big bite of it.

"Mmm….mmm…This fruit has the pleasant smell of a blooming rose," the youngster said and added, "I think I'll have another bite before I can really tell what it is."

He took another big bite and another and another and each time, he would say, "Mmm..Mmm…It's very tender…. Mmm…Mmm… It's very sweet….Mmm…Mmm….It's very juicy."

Alas, when he said, "Mmm…Mmm…It's very delicious. I love it very much.", the fruit was already reduced to a mere knob and had yet to be identified.

The cunning youngster got to eat the whole fruit and when he left, the three foolish men even gave him the presents and were apologetic when the youngster claimed that they had been late for his party and that all his guests had gone home.

The three foolish men were justly called foolish, don't you think?

8

The Truth About Little Miss Cootie

It would be very unlikely that you have heard about little Miss Cootie. Most probably, you would think that someone with such a strange name would surely come from a very exotic land in a faraway corner of the earth which of course, would not be true if you have in your mind, a little girl from a place as ancient and exotic as India or China or one with a name you may find difficulty in pronouncing like Uzbekistan or Czechoslovakia. No parents in their right minds would also name their daughter, 'Cootie' for it really sounds weird since it sounds more like some kinds of birds and then some bullies in school might start calling 'Miss Cootie', 'Coolie' or 'Cookie' which of course would not be very nice at all.

Miss Cootie, of course, was not your average kind of girl. She was actually a fairy; and being very little, was called 'Little Miss Cootie' by people who knew her. Her size was really not larger than the biggest bumblebee in the garden and since Little Miss Cootie had also a pair of silvery wings and was always flying here and there in her yellow and black striped jumper, she was often mistaken for a bee herself!

Weng Leong and his sister had their first encounter with Little Miss Cootie one day when they were out in the garden catching butterflies. Weng Leong's sister had mistaken the fairy as a little butterfly and had only managed to land her after numerous scoops with her net. You could just imagine what a terrible time poor Little Miss Cootie had! There were butterflies indeed on her tummy as she flew quickly, left and right, up and down and round and round to avoid being caught!

Little Miss Cootie would probably have flown off when the first opportunity to escape arose but one of her wings had torn off slightly when Weng Leong's sister fumbled in extricating her from the net. To her further chagrin, she was roughly pushed into a hot, stuffy glass jar that reeked of sour pineapple!

How surprised the siblings were when they realized that the insect that was yelling in the jam jar was but a winged little girl in a striped jumper! They wasted no time at all in nursing her and catering to her fancy!

Ah! Imagine the things people would do for fairies!

Weng Leong and his sister fed Little Miss Cootie with the choicest food. They kept the fairy in Weng Leong's room upstairs and did not complain at all even when they had to climb up and down the stairs a million times to fetch whatever food that Little Miss Cootie bided. Often, the fairy would not even finish the food that she asked for and the siblings would find themselves fighting over the leftovers since they rather like the idea of eating the food that had been consumed by fairies!

Little Miss Cootie grew well in no time and got rather plump too! When her wings healed, she just flew off through the window, back to her heavenly abode in the garden.

The siblings did not see Little Miss Cootie again and never did they really find out the reason why she left.

The truth was simply that Little Miss Cootie was such a health-conscious fairy that she was beginning to worry about her blood cholesterol level the minute she realized that she was getting too plump with all the good food heaped on her. It was not that she mind the attention but health, to her, come first.

And then of course, you would not have suspected that all these while, she had purposely made the two siblings go up and down the stairs to do her bidding. She was rather cross with them for catching her in the first place and then, for damaging her wings and putting her in a horrible jam jar. She had planned her revenge and executed it in her own sweet time. So, you'd say it was sweet revenge all the way throughout the time when Little Miss Cootie was recuperating and you know, you should see how her eyes glinted when the siblings fought over the leftovers.

How malicious a little fairy could be!

9

A House Divided

Old Mr. Goh sat up suddenly in his bed. There was such a commotion upstair.

Just the other morning, Old Mr. Goh was collecting eggs to be sold in the market when he thought he heard a sweet voice behind him.

"Aren't you lonely staying all alone in your big house?" The voice queried and then suggested, "Wouldn't you like it if I move into one of the empty rooms in your house to keep you company?"

Old Mr. Goh turned around and was surprised to be confronted by a white mother hen with a bright red comb. The blue eyes of the hen pierced old Mr. Goh's as if demanding an answer to a question asked.

When it seemed that there was no forthcoming answer, the hen clucked furiously. "Yes, it's me talking to you!" She said.

An egg Old Mr. Goh was holding immediately fell from his grasp and broke on hitting the floor.

"There, there…Such a good egg has gone to waste," the mother hen then said in a kinder tone. She was such a smooth talker that she talked herself into being given a room of her own in Old Mr. Goh's house!

And the mother hen was not the only talking animal that Old Mr. Goh encountered that day!

Not long after the hen moved into her room, a strange animal with a big pocket across his abdomen hopped into the living room on his two hind legs!

"You must give me shelter!" The greyish creature begged of Old Mr. Goh. "I just have to escape somewhere," he said. "I can't live with dumb animals in cages!"

Old Mr. Goh took the animal in and that perhaps, was a mistake!

The newcomer took an instant liking of his new home. He liked the sweet green shrubs that grew in abundance around the area and loved to hop especially up the wooden stairs since it made such a terribly loud booming sound that he found so pleasing to his ears.

While the mother hen did not find fault with the animal over food since she took solely paddy grains, she could not help getting irritated over the noise that the animal made when he hopped up the stairs, which was really, rather often.

Very soon, both animals were not on talking terms. When they did talk, they would always end up in a quarrel and created such din that it gave Old Mr. Goh splitting headaches and sleepless nights!

Old Mr. Goh would often lay motionless in bed each night as he worried over the two talking animals. Animals apparently could not live together under the same roof!

The animals were at it again. In the wee, wee morning, Old Mr. Goh could hear the mother hen kicking up a fuss. She was running all over the place upstairs, flapping her wings and clucking hysterically. Something was chasing her round and round.

When the clucking stopped abruptly, it crossed Old Mr. Goh's mind that perhaps, the feud between the mother hen and the animal would end right there and then; and perhaps, it would end brutally and even fatally!

That really sent shivers down Old Mr. Goh's spine!

Old Mr. Goh rushed instantly upstairs to check on the animals.

When he entered the mother hen's room, he was surprised to see her sitting as quietly as a mouse in the pocket of her arch-enemy!

A bruised fox had just jumped out through the window.

Old Mr. Goh's house most probably would not stand divided no more. That would be if the mother hen was grateful enough to appreciate the animal that had saved her from the fox.

Animals normally are not grateful.

10

Pinkie Wanted To Be In The Circus

Pinkie had dreamed of being in the circus ever since she could remember. Her mommy and daddy had brought her to the circus when she was barely four and she could still recall that terrific day when the crowd was mesmerized by a little elephant as old as Pinkie, performing a balancing trick on a big red ball. Pinkie would simply welcome such adoration herself!

The circus had come to town again! It had got Pinkie terribly excited! Her mommy and daddy had promised to take her again to the circus and this time, she would not be sitting on mommy's lap. She would get a seat all to herself! She would be sitting in the front row and if she could help it, she would not be again lapping away greedily at the sugar cane juice that came in a paper cup! If she was lucky, the circus owner might even notice her and want her to be in the circus!

Pinkie would have to know some tricks! She would love to balance herself on a big red ball but when she tried that the last time on her brother's blue rubber ball, it burst with a loud bang and she fell flat on her face! She was badly bruised and severely reprimanded!

Pinkie knew a few interesting card tricks that her daddy had taught her but that would not be good enough! She would have to know something better like contorting her body or performing some tricks in the air like those daring trapeze artistes whom she had seen performing in television if she really wanted to turn professional but then, she really had difficulty even in bending her big hard body when she did her daily stretch exercises and boy, was she really afraid of heights! It always made her head dizzy and she would have goose pimples all over her body!

Pinkie had to think of something pretty fast! She would be going to the circus that night and if the circus owner happened to notice her, she would want to show him her skills!

Some friends of Pinkie's mommy would come over for tea in the afternoon. Pinkie's mother served them some home-made yam cakes and soya bean juice and when they left, there was a pile of dirty dishes, plates and cups to be washed.

Pinkie helped her mommy with the washing up and it was then that an idea crossed her mind! If only she could whirl the dishes and plates on the tip of her fiddler stick!

Pinkie spent the rest of the afternoon in her room, practising to balance the dishes and plates! She practised very hard but by evening, she had only managed to break all the dishes and plates! What a big disappointment the whole affair was!

Pinkie's mommy had ushered her to get ready for the circus!

With a big sigh, Pinkie put on her pink frilly outfit. She put on a matching big pink ribbon on her head and applied some very thick mascara on her face. Then, she applied some very dark blue eye shadows on her eyelids and added a dash of glitter before putting on the false eyelashes! She really looked very cute and really, really stood out in the crowd when she put on her pink high heels and carried the little pink handbag which her mommy had bought her for her tenth birthday. Everyone who came to the circus noticed her and could not help laughing!

"Ho! Ho! Ho!" The circus owner roared as tears rolled down his eyes. "What a funny little elephant you are! You would make a very good clown!"

Thus began Pinkie's legendary career as an elephant clown!

11

Celebration Of Life

Siok Mooi and her parents were on holiday to an exotic country. They were visiting a tribal village in a remote mountainous area. When the four-wheel drive they were travelling in, moved to a gradual halt on the dusty road, a group of brown-skinned dishevelled looking children started to crowd round them, asking for money.

The tourist guide told Siok Mooi and her parents to ignore the children.

"Don't give them anything," the tourist guide said. "You'll not help anyone by giving handouts."

A brown-skinned woman with nearly ten brass rings encircling her long slender neck and huge iron earrings dangling heavily from her long earlobes smiled as if in approval of the tourist guide. She was clad in a bright red traditional costume and her smile revealed teeth stained with betel nut juice.

The woman muttered something to the tourist guide in her own strange dialect before leading the group down the road.

"We are all in luck," the tourist guide said. "I have been told that there is some kind of celebration in the village."

People in the village were singing. Drums and cymbals were beaten. Of course, there was a celebration for there was a new baby in the gaily-decorated house that Siok Mooi and her parents were brought to. Green streamers dangling from the ceiling swayed in the wind as if to welcome them and green crepe papers cut out into beautiful designs had been pasted on every door to indicate that there was birth in the house.

"The birth of a baby marks the beginning of life. It is a joyous occasion and calls for much celebration," the tourist guide said just as a chubby brown baby was taken out from its green cot to be admired by visitors.

"Isn't the baby cute?" The tourist guide then asked.

"There must be many more other new babies in the other houses," Siok Mooi said. She had noticed that the house opposite was as gaily decorated.

"No...no.... as a matter of fact, not every house has a new baby," the tourist guide said and explained, "There are other celebrations. A boy in the house opposite had just reached the age of puberty and the family is celebrating now that he is becoming aware of his responsibility as a human being."

The second house had red streamers dangling from its ceiling and red paper cuttings pasted on the doors. The boy who was on the threshold of manhood was attired fully in red and was placed on a dais of the same hue. Children round him were dressed in traditional costumes and they sang songs and exchanged repartee.

"The boy would have to earn his right to celebrate the next chapter of his life," The tourist guide said. "Just like the eighty year old lady next door. As a maiden, she cared for her husband and children, toiling in the paddy field; and now that she has become old and feeble, adoring children and grandchildren crowd round her feet, waiting to bathe her with scented water and feed her with honey." Her house had yellow streamers and yellow paper cuttings.

There was a loud commotion when Siok Mooi and her parents walked up the stairs to her house. Little children started to wail loudly while women with moist eyes were beating their chest in anguish.

The grand old lady of the house with the yellow streamers and yellow paper cuttings had suddenly breathed her last.

"Surely this will not call for a celebration," Siok Mooi thought.

A flurry of activities began to unfold in the house. The yellow streamers and paper cuttings were pulled down quickly and replaced with purple ones. A horn was blown and a group of women started to chant in unison. Neighbours who heard the sound of the horn flocked immediately to the house, bearing fresh flowers for the deceased.

When a loved one leaves suddenly and in a way that nature demands, you may think that the deceased will go on to meet her Creator or her Ancestor or even go on to live a new life as an animal or another person. Either way, it is a joyous occasion. It is nice to be able to thank one's Creator personally for all the joys one has and to be able to talk about old times with one's Ancestor and of course, leading a new life as another being means getting another shot at life. There is nothing to fear if a life is well lived since then, there are only good things ahead.

Turning to Siok Mooi, the tourist guide had said, "You were luckier than I had thought. At such a tender age, you'd get to see how life is celebrated."

Knowing life, one will never mourn.

12

Little Women

Maxi was having a sweet dream when her mother's voice woke her up from her slumber. Maxi had dreamed that she was Hafaezah, the lovely village maiden. Maxi loved the idea of being a woman, more so a beautiful and popular one like Hafaezah.

"I am going to be a woman someday, mom," Maxi told her mother as she got up from her bed. "I'm going to be like Hafaezah, the beautiful lady living below our house. I am going to call myself Fatimah and I'll get to wear a beautiful red *sarong kebaya*. I'll be as glamorous as any other woman can be." She said with a twinkle in her eyes. Her long, thin tail began to wag, as pleased as can be.

Maxi had a tail for she was a little brown female mouse just dreaming to be a human being.

Midi, another brown female mouse sharing her dream, had popped over at Maxi's house for a chat.

"Hey, did you hear the humans in the house talking about a powerful sorceress living in the woods?" Midi asked.

"They say many village maidens have sought her help to make them attractive."

The mention of the sorceress made Maxi sit up with a start.

"Does she know a lot of magic?" Maxi asked excitedly. "Can she transform mice into human beings?"

"Well, I don't know… but I did hear that she makes magic potions out of our kinds," Midi replied.

That probably put an end to Maxi's interest in the sorceress.

Later that evening, when Maxi and Midi were trying to get their paws on some bread in a rattan basket, they felt the basket they were in, moved suddenly.

Hafaezah had got hold of the basket and she was heading towards the woods. She was going to pay the sorceress a visit!

Maxi and Midi hid themselves under some old newspaper that lined the bottom of the basket. Through a hole, they could see clearly a little old wrinkled woman hunching over a cauldron overflowing with a boiling green liquid.

Hafaezah had walked into the hut of the sorceress who made magic potions out of rats!

Maxi and Midi shuddered when the sorceress's dark eyes pierced into the basket.

"Thank you for bringing the food, Hafaezah," the sorceress said as she took the bread from the basket and placed them on a tray near some weird looking mushrooms which she had gathered from the forest. She then ladled some green liquid from the cauldron and filled it into a glass bottle.

Putting the bottle into the basket, the sorceress had then said, "This newly concocted vegetarian magic potion is for you, Hafaezah. One just has to take a sip to make one's dream come true."

When Hafaezah was on her way home, Maxi and Midi came excitedly out of their hiding place to steal a sip of the magic potion. Their dream of becoming human beings immediately came true!

You'd think that Hafaezah would be disappointed to find her magic potion gone when she got home. Well, she would be terrified too, if she find two very little women in her basket for that was what Maxi and Midi had become after taking the magic potion!

13

A Still Forest Pool

Jui Miang fell asleep during Maths lesson. His Math teacher woke him up with a sharp tap on his shoulder and then kept close tab on him for the next thirty minutes. Poor Jui Miang! He had a hard time keeping his eyes open.

The day was particularly hot. The ceiling fan in the classroom was not working and the room hemmed in by dusty long curtains with gaudy colours, had become extremely stuffy and humid. The triangles on the green board had seemed to swim before his eyes and he had much difficulty in following the lesson on trigonometry.

Jui Miang heaved a big sigh of relief when the school bell finally rang to mark the end of the Math period. When the Maths teacher left, he grabbed his satchel bag and started to leave the class.

It was half past twelve the students from the afternoon session were creating quite a din outside. The History teacher would be attending another one of those long teachers' meeting and classes would be as usual, left unattended. Students almost always had a gala time then and some like Jui Miang had found it to be just the perfect time to play truant.

Jui Miang mingled with the big crowd of students from the afternoon session and before long, had walked past the school gate unnoticed by the school authorities.

He walked quickly along a narrow laterite lane.

The sun was scorching hot and Jui Miang, being drowsy from an overdose of late night TV shows, had decided to take a break under the shade of a big *angsana* tree that stood beside a still blue pool.

Jui Miang had wandered deep into a forest but he was too tired and sleepy to care. He stretched himself on a big slab of granite rock to catch a wink and even made a pillow out of his school bag!

Jui Miang could feel his entire body reverberate and it felt extremely soothing when a cool breeze blew forth from the still forest pool.

The breeze blew the pink blooms of the *angsana tree* from their branches and they fell like gentle raindrops on Jui Miang, almost burying him from head to toe.

As Jui Miang lay thus on the slab of granite rock, a ripple started to form on the still water in the centre of the blue pool.

Two little round eyes then popped up suddenly and they started to rotate as if to survey the area.

Satisfied that the place was deserted, a big black crab had flipped itself up onto the slab of granite rock right in front of where Jui Miang was dozing!

"Come on, my friends," the big black crab whistled and said, "There's no one around. Hop onto this slab of rock at once and let's party!"

The next instant, crabs of various sizes and hues were flipping out of the still forest pool. There were big crabs, medium sized crabs, small crabs, blue crabs, green crabs, pink, purple crabs and even hairy crabs and crabs with colourful stripes!

The crabs seemed to rejoice at the opportunity of getting away from their watery abode. They started to dance on the slab of granite rock as if it was a stage, filling the forest with a click-clack sound.

A little blue crab stepped accidentally on Jui Miang's toe, causing him to stir.

The crab turned white immediately and burst our crying.

"Boo-hoo-hoo! There is a boy sleeping on the rock!" It wailed.

A big blue crab promptly came forward and pinched Jui Miang so hard that he jumped up with a scream.

All the other crabs stopped dancing immediately and began to pinch Jui Miang on the feet, legs, body and face.

Poor Jui Miang! He had to run for his dear life!

When Jui Miang reached home, his school uniform was in tatters and he had bruises all over his body. Nobody would believe that crabs had attacked him and that there were crabs in the still forest pool.

His father even spanked him for playing truant!

14

Hair

If anyone has any hair problem, it would probably not be as serious as that faced by Shir Li and her sister, Shir Fen. Their problems started on Monday afternoon when Shir Li took a public bus home from school. The bus was particularly crowded then but Shir Li thought she was lucky indeed to have a seat even though she had to sit beside another older unfriendly looking girl who had a dirty mop of curly hair.

When Shir Li alighted from the bus, she felt a slight itch on her head. She gave her head a slight scratch and thought the itchiness would go away.

After taking a bath, Shir Li however continued to feel the itchiness on her head. She scratched it when she was taking her lunch and her mother could not help but reprimand, "Stop scratching your head, girl!"

Shir Li continued to scratch her head right through the day when she was doing her homework, watching TV, having dinner and even after she had jumped into the bed, which she shared with Shir Fen. She did not get a good night sleep, of course, for she would wake up occasionally to scratch away the growing itchiness on her head.

The next morning, Shir Li was not the only one scratching her head at the breakfast table. Shir Fen had picked up the habit and it irked their mother terribly to see both her girls scratching their heads.

She could not help but scold, "Stop scratching your heads, girls!"

Both the girls however, could not heed their mother.

They continued to scratch their heads when they were in their school bus and went on scratching them throughout the day when they were in school. They had a hard time then since almost all the teachers in class embarrassed them by asking them to stop scratching their heads. Their classmates had even thought they were both acting like monkeys!

When the girls failed to stop scratching their heads, their mother decided to do something about it. She started pouring some kerosene on the girls' heads, which of course, alarmed the girls greatly. Then, after their mother had wrapped their kerosene-doused hair with coconut husks, they just cringed to a corner. They just squatted there silently as they waited for the worst fate could deal them.

How pitiful the sisters had looked then! They could not help but wondered if their mother would light a match and set their hair on fire!

Shir Li and Shir Fen kept on scratching their heads even after their mother had removed the coconut husks from their heads and washed their hair for the umpteen times.

Driven to her wits end, their mother had decided to take them to an Indian barber at the back of their house to have their long locks cut off!

How horrified the sisters were! They could not imagine having to go to the barber's; let alone, going bald!

The sisters were practically crying when they were at the barber's.

The kind Indian barber tried to pacify them and when he looked at their hair, he just turned to their mother and said, "I haven't seen so many lice in anyone's hair before! They are practically crawling all over!"

The Indian barber then began to sharpen his scissors. As he was doing that, he said, "Madam, are you sure you want me to cut off your daughters' hair? You can get some special shampoo from the local clinic to kill the lice, you know. You can still save your daughters' crowning glory."

Shir Li and Shir Fen would thank the Indian barber days later. Upon his advice, the lice in their hair were finally got rid off and they got to keep their hair.

As for Shir Li, she would never ever sit beside anyone with dirty hair again for she was sure the lice in her hair were from the girl whom she sat with in the bus.

And she made sure too that she had had her hair shampooed everyday!

15

Four Animals In A Car

One day, a mischievous long tailed grey haired monkey came down from its home atop a rain tree to search for food. Coming down, it was surprised to find a blue car parked in a very haphazard manner. A door of the car was ajar and there was a bunch of golden yellow banana in a red plastic basket inside.

"Aha! That's just what I need to tuck in!" The monkey thought to itself. "How lucky am I today!"

Smiling quietly at its good fortune, the monkey had without much hesitation, jumped into the back of the car where the basket of banana was. It was about to lay its paws on a banana when the door suddenly slammed shut behind it.

A middle-aged man in a yellow round collar T-shirt and a pair of faded blue jeans had appeared from nowhere to shut the door. Oblivious of the monkey, he had proceeded to jump into the driver's seat and had fumbled to turn on the ignition key. The man, who was reeking of alcohol, had red bleary eyes and was obviously drunk. He managed to start the engine and went on to drive west towards the town centre.

It was barely minutes after the car had sped off when the monkey heard the drunken man mumbled to himself, "Ah! An orange ball had just rolled across the road!"

"That's just what little Danny had been pestering me to buy all afternoon," he said and stepped on the brake abruptly, throwing both the monkey and the plastic red basket off-balance.

A little white kitten fell out from the basket but it failed to catch the attention of the drunken man. The latter was already out of the car and was on the road, trying very hard to catch the rolling ball. He had to run very hard after the ball and when he finally caught it, he was far too drunk to realize that it was merely a big fat hen!

The drunken man carried the big fat hen back towards the car.

Just then, a black goat trotted by. A long rope was trailing from its neck.

"Ah! I see little Danny's pet dog had run away from home!" The man in his drunkenness mumbled and proceeded to catch hold of the rope with his other free hand. He led the reluctant goat to the car where he threw both hen and goat into the back seat.

There were now four animal passengers at the back of the car!

"Cluck! Cluck! I want to get back to my coop and be with my friends before they miss me!" The orange hen said anxiously.

"Bah! The black goat fumed. "I should be with my friends, too; enjoying those tender grass shoots by the lake!"

The monkey which had taken its fill of the bananas, had wanted to make for home too.

"I know what we should do," the monkey said and then suggested to the hen and the goat, "If both of you can knock the drunken man unconscious, I will tie him up with this long rope that you have here on your neck!"

The orange hen thus began to peck at the drunken man and the goat jumped to butt him out of his senses!

After the monkey had tied up the drunken man, it went on to open the door of the car to let the other animals out.

"We are all leaving here this instance," the monkey announced and then turned to ask the little white kitten, "What are you going to do?"

The little kitten, in turn, merely jumped back into the red plastic basket and purred, "I guess I'll just have to go back to sleep for a little while longer. I hope when I wake up, my master would be wide awake and sober enough to drive me home!"

The three animals therefore left the little white kitten all alone in the car with the senseless drunken man!

16

Testimony Of Two Wallets

A brown and black wallet met for the first time when they were summoned to court. While waiting for their turns to testify, both had sat on the same bench and struck up a conversation.

"Hello," the brown wallet had greeted to break the ice. "Are you here in court today to be a witness to some wrong doing?" He asked.

The black wallet nodded and being very talkative, had offered his whole story without much prodding.

"My master is a young man of about thirty," the black wallet started his story. "He was riding his motorcycle to the supermarket when I slipped out from the back pocket of his old blue jeans. He was not aware of that, of course, until very much later when he was at the supermarket, trying to get me out to pay the cashier for something he had bought. It was then that he realized that I was gone. Immediately he went back to search for me but to no avail. Another older man had already picked me up from the hard tarred road. The latter had obviously seen me falling but made no attempt to call out to my master."

"It is not a case of a wallet being snatched then," the brown wallet concluded. "I have heard of cases where women were hurt when thieves snatched their handbags. Recently, a victim fell into a coma when she fell from her bicycle and knocked her head. The thief had left her there to die after stealing her bag."

"Poor woman!" The black wallet then said, "I bet her family must be grieving. If human beings could only be like us wallets…We don't rob and steal and we are always generous with our money when we have it and just as satisfied when we don't."

"Anyway," The black wallet then continued his story, "The older man who picked me up, relieved me of all my money and threw away my master's personal documents. He even had the cheek to try to use the bank card to withdraw my master's hard-earned money. He failed to do that, of course, and I am glad he was caught."

"And what is your story?" The black wallet asked the brown wallet. "Why are you in court today?"

"Mine is totally a different story," the brown wallet said. "My master is supposed to be a bright teenager of about seventeen. He lost me when he was alighting from a school bus. Nobody saw me fall and I lay on the road until very late in the evening.

A middle-aged woman found me and being the honest woman she was, she left my money intact. She checked my master's documents and traced him to his house. She went to see him that very night at about ten to return me.

When she asked to see my master however, the latter refused to budge from his room since the former was all but a stranger.

Of course, he did come out finally, after much coaxing and after learning that the woman was there to return his wallet.

He had put on a sour face then as he had been busy doing his school work and was not happy at being interrupted. He went through me and finding nothing missing, he just walked off without as much as a smile or a simple thank you."

"It's a case of a rude brat?" the black wallet asked.

"I suppose so. The boy had been sued for being insolent," the brown wallet had managed to say just before the judge appeared and the court session began.

17

A Cute Little Bunny

When Poh Chin visited his uncle, he was pleased to be given a room all to himself.

Flinging his bag into a chair and jumping straight into a blue velvety bed, he felt the bed rippled like water and for a euphoric moment, he thought he was indeed somewhere in the garden of Eden!

Poh Chin pressed the 'On' button of a remote control which he found lying on the table.

A television screen facing him, immediately sizzled into a big gaping hole.

Thud! Thud! Thud!

The room seemed to reverberate when bunnies hopping out of the hole, landed paws first on the hard terrazzo floor.

In no time at all, the room was swarmed with bunnies. There must be hundreds of them – bright orange bunnies with soft curly fur! They nibbled away at the furniture and went on to build a miniature bunny town!

A cute little bunny dressed in a school uniform and with a satchel bag hanging on his shoulder, rubbed his head amiably on Poh Chn's shin.

When Poh Chin looked down, the blue-eyed bunny asked, "Would you like to come home with me?"

"But how could I?" Poh Chin stammered back. "I am too big to even walk down the street!" He said.

The bunny said that Poh Chin needed only to have the desire and since he did have that, he immediately shrunk and became so small that the bunny appeared to him to be like a giant!

Poh Chin raced after the bunny down the street lined with bright yellow, blooming hibiscus shrubs, taking in the scene of the quaint bunny town until he came to a little cosy cottage with a red chimney.

Mummy bunny, still donning her apron and with a wooden ladle on her paw, was standing at the door.

"What do you bring home this time, young bunny?" She asked sternly as she rested her paws on her hip.

"This pitiful boy followed me all the way home, Mummy," the little bunny declared earnestly, "He was gibbering when I found him all lost and alone in the street."

"Can I keep him, please?" He then pleaded. "He can sleep in my room. I have a paper box big enough for his bed. I'll put rags and old newspapers in it to keep him warm and cosy and when he is hungry, I'll give him some *boy* biscuits!"

Mummy Bunny threw Poh Chin a quick glance.

Nodding her head slowly, she said, "All right, but you must promise to bathe him regularly, toilets train him and take him out to exercise."

"Yippee!" The little bunny yelled with delight and hopped to peck his mother on her cheek.

"Don't be so happy yet, dear," his mother reminded. "He'll have to go if he runs all over the place. You'd better get him a leash."

Poh Chin shrieked his protest.

Picking him up by his neck, the little bunny said, "You are getting gibberish again!" He had then tried to undress Poh Chin for a bath when he was bitten on the paw!

Poh Chin ran quickly out of the front door and made good his escape into the street. He found refuge behind a shady hibiscus shrub. Trembling, he groped and managed to find the remote control in his pocket.

When he pressed its 'Off' button, there was a loud sizzling sound.

The big gaping black hole in his room had turned back into a television screen.

Sometimes, strange things happened when Poh Chin got too engrossed with watching the home videos. In this case, his life was almost taken over.

18

Magic Slippers

Have you ever been to a supermarket and got smitten with something there? Twelve-year –old Guo Kang had. One day, when he was out with his friends in the supermarket in town, they wandered off to the shoes section and there on the shelf was a pair of pink slippers with white polka dots. The slippers were the cutest that Guo Kang had ever seen. It had a pair of long ears, bulging eyes and white whiskers and looked very much like the rabbit he had seen in a cartoon programme in television, only that it lacked feet and a tail and had for a nose, a big black button.

Guo Kang simply must have the slippers! Without much thought, he splurged all the thirty dollars that he had saved for months.

Guo Kang was very much pleased with his buy especially when the slippers drew gasps of admiration from all at home. His mother loved the slippers even though she was of the opinion their soles were far too soft and could probably not last long. So, Guo Kang kept his slippers under lock and key, never even intending to wear them at all!

However, that night when he slipped into the slippers for fun, he felt a strange tingling sensation on his feet. His muscles seemed to relax instantly and he found himself prancing around his room! He was just like a lively little foal in a vast green meadow!

Guo Kang would break into a somersault or roll on the floor every now and then and before he realized it, suddenly, he had begun tap dancing and was soon already tap dancing away for one solid hour! He was tapping away like a professional and was he surprised with himself indeed!

When the clock struck twelve, Guo Kang found himself skipping out into the living room and out through its open window! There in the garden, a layer of thick mist had carpeted the lawn and there were all kinds of bunny slippers imaginable, tapping and dancing away in the moonlight!

Guo Kang found himself dancing away with the slippers. For a while, he thought he was the only human there.

Then, he heard a sweet voice like a bell behind him.

He turned around to see a cute little girl in a white frilly frock and a matching little white ribbon on her mop of curly hair. The girl had rosy, chubby cheeks which broke into two cute little dimples when she smiled and introduced herself.

Shirley who was wearing the same pink bunny slippers with white polka dots, danced away like a pro! She was a perfect dancing partner for Guo Kang and oh! How the two danced away into the wee, wee morning!

When the first ray of sunlight appeared from behind the distant hills, Shirley asked to be excused. She was afraid that her parents would miss her.

While Guo Kang was reluctant to part company, he could feel the magical tingling sensation on his feet diminishing and he had also begun feeling a bit tired. The magic slippers had also begun to drag him on his feet, back to his bedroom where upon hitting bed, he fell instantly into a deep slumber.

Guo Kang woke up very late that day. He woke up, aching all over the body but he still looked forward to slipping into his magic slippers again.

He was hoping to return the little white ribbon, which he had found in the garden to its rightful owner.

19

A Little Secret Garden

ChinChi loved it each time his mother took him over to his auntie's house. During tea, when his mother chatted with Aunty Yen Yen, there would always be tasty peanut cookies for him to chomp on. When he had taken enough of his fill, Chin Chi would then storm off to the little manicured garden in the backyard.

There, Chin Chi would as if in frenzy, run round and round, bare-footed. He loved the feel of the soft grass and the slap of the gentle breeze on his cheeks.

Chin Chi wished he had a garden of his own!

Chin Chi lived in a little fishing village. His house was at the estuary and it stood on very high stilts to avoid getting wet by the water, which never fail to rise and fall each day with the tide. There was hardly any land for Chin Chi to have even a small garden!

When Chin Chi got home from a visit to Aunty Yen Yen's house on Saturday, he had caught sight of some discarded planks in front of his house. Chin Chi immediately thought of salvaging them for a plan that flashed suddenly in his mind. He would make his own little garden!

Borrowing a hammer, a saw and some nails from his father, Chin Chi proceeded to make a little wooden box, not bigger than the drawer of his study table. He filled the box with earth, which he bought for two dollars a packet from the nursery and sprinkled on the surface, some balsam seeds a classmate had given him.

Chin Chi kept the box in his room, beside the aquarium where he kept a pair of his pet green tortoises. He left it at the window sill so that there will be enough sunlight. There! Chin Chi was going to have his own little garden! If he did not tell anyone about it, you could say the little boy had a little secret garden of his own!

Chin Chi smiled to himself at the thought of having a little secret garden. He was rather pleased to have come up with the idea of growing flowers in a box in the first place, and was doubly pleased to think of the pleasure it would bring in days to come. His window sill would, before long, be splashed with red, pink, purple and the myriad of colours would make the fishermen's heads turn when they sail past in their fishing boats. His own parents would also be pleasantly surprised!

Chin Chi watered his little garden diligently each day and looked forward to the first green sprout. Day after day, he watered and waited and when there was no sign of a new life coming out of the box, he thought he had planted some bad balsam seeds He tried his luck again with some other seeds but was dismayed to face the same results.

Unknown to Chin Chi, each night when he was fast asleep in his cosy bed, a pair of little imps from the river would hop straight into his flower box through the open window. The water imps loved to frolic in the soft, damp earth and were extremely delighted to find in them, tasty and crunchy seeds! They fed on the seeds and that was the reason why the plants failed to grow!

Chin Chi's luck only changed when he switched to growing cactus.

The next time the water imps jumped into the box, they landed on the cactus and their buttocks were severely pricked!

"Ouch! Ouch!" The two imps could not help shouting out loudly, waking up Chin Chi in the process. The latter, however, was too sleepy to even care. He heard one splash after another when the imps jumped backed into the river but thought nothing about it.

As for the water imps, they never returned to the flower box again.

20

A Wedding Feast

Tommy called the bare spacious hole in an old *meranti* tree, home. Being an orphan squirrel, he lived alone, a simple carefree life devoid of responsibility.

One cold morning, Tommy woke up from a heavy slumber to find his home illuminated by a strange green glow.

A firefly had flown into his home!

"Oh, dear! I can't make it home on time and I'm beat! Can you let me rest here till I get my strength back, kind squirrel?" The little firefly asked.

Before Tommy could reply, a black and white magpie flew in.

"Excuse me, kind squirrel," The magpie said and panted, "Can I take refuge in your house? A big bad boy outside is trying to shoot me down with his catapult!"

Tommy took pity on the two creatures. He allowed them to stay in his house as long as they liked.

Later, after both the firefly and the magpie had left, Tommy hopped out from his home to hunt for nuts. He jumped head on into a warm, furry animal and almost froze with fright!

It was just a dainty female squirrel which had just moved into the neighbourhood!

Tommy had seen Daisy a number of times when he hopped past her house in the *Jelutung* tree by the river and he had long been smitten!

The two squirrels became firm friends after their close brush with each other and before long, wedding bells were ringing!

From a simply carefree squirrel, Tommy transformed overnight into a mature squirrel filled with responsibility.

Tommy had big plans for Daisy. He was going to throw a huge wedding feast attended by all the squirrels in the woods just to thrill her! He went on to carve a new home in a hard teak tree for himself and Daisy to live in. He decorated it with wild flowers and filled the larder with Daisy's favourite nuts.

The firefly and magpie would later help made the wedding feast memorable.

When Tommy wedded Daisy, their wedding feast was held atop the teak tree where their love nest was. It was held at night when there was a full moon. The teak tree looked like one giant Christmas tree when it was lighted up by a million fireflies roped in by Tommy's little firefly friend. A million magpies had also been roped in by his Magpie friend to serenade the happy couple on their special day.

Friends make you happy in ways you least expect!

21

Rainbow In Her Heart

Mrs. Lim watched her six-year-old daughter, Meow San intently as the latter admired some flowers in a vase.

"It's springtime again," The thin little girl said as she drank in the beautiful sight of the red roses.

"The roses are in full bloom and just look at those beautiful butterflies out to gather their nectar," Meow San said as she held out her hands as if to touch the butterflies.

Of course, it was not spring. The weather had always been hot and humid and there would never be spring, summer, autumn or winter, let alone butterflies in a drab hospital room that smelled of anaesthetics.

Meow San had however, always been a cheerful and imaginative girl as far as Mrs. Lim could remember. A cold day would be winter to her and then, she would be busy building a snowman out of some white cotton in the house. Every other hot day would be summer and sometimes, she would be found sunbathing in the garden where yellow leaves there reminded her of her favourite season, autumn.

Meow San indeed was an unusual girl. Unlike others who always complained of one thing or another about everything, she was the rare one who would always see something good in them.

As both mother and daughter stared at the pouring rain through the glass window, the elderly woman could not help but shed a tear.

"Don't cry, mummy." Meow San then said as she crept into her mother's lap. She caressed Mrs. Lim's cheek with her little hand and gave her a gentle peck there as she whispered, "There is going to be a rainbow after the rain. You just wait. When the sky clears, the sun would shine and turn all the little droplets of water outside into twinkling diamonds. The birds would then come out to sing while pretty girls like me would dance. There would also be a big pot of gold at the end of the rainbow!"

Mrs. Lim managed to smile a little when little Meow San added, "Of course, the pot of gold is immaterial. It is there merely to distract you from everything that is real and beautiful. You will be happy enough if you just sit still and watch the multi-hued rainbow cutting across the blue sky, funnelling true happiness from heaven."

Mrs. Lim had probably not been smiling for a very long time. She had been extremely worried ever since the day Meow San had a nasty fall down the stair. The latter had earlier been complaining of dizzy spells and Mrs. Lim was just taking her to her family doctor for a check-up when the accident happened.

Meow San had a severe cut on the forehead. She lost a large amount of blood and had to be rushed to the hospital where she was given blood transfusion. The cut had left her with an ugly scar, which she could not conceal with her hair since she had long been suffering from *alopecia*, a baldness caused by an allergy to the chemicals released by her hair follicles.

Suffering from *alopecia* was not such a big problem since the doctor had told Mrs. Lim that Meow San would have her long, silky hair back when she reach puberty during which time her chemical makeup would change. What had hurt Mrs. Lim most was during the blood transfusion; her precious daughter had been given blood contaminated with the AIDs virus.

Mrs. Lim could not help but marvelled at her daughter.

As the little girl wasted her body away in the hospital bed, the girl was still formidable in spirit and had continued to be alert in her mind. She was cheerful most of the time and her cheerfulness rubbed off on those who were near her.

There was no doubt a rainbow in the little girl's heart, funnelling happiness from where heaven was. Her short life on earth was undoubtedly a time well spent and for this, Mrs. Lim found solace.

22

The Pencil Case

Yek Ling was going through his birthday presents. He unwrapped a green box and found in it, a yellow lion. His uncle had given him a soft toy for his birthday! The lion had a long tail, four stubby legs and a brown mane. There was a zipper running across the lion's back. When Yek Ling unzipped the zipper, he found pens, pencils, erasers and a red sharpener inside. It was actually a pencil case that his uncle had given him! It was a special pencil case in the form of a cute little lion!

Yek Ling was rather pleased with his new pencil case. He took it to school the next morning and placed it on his desk for all to see. Later, when he wanted to copy the history notes on the whiteboard, he decided to use a pen from it.

Yek Ling reached for the pencil case.

Just as he was about to get hold of it, he heard a gruff voice roared. "Oh, no, you don't! Don't think you are going to get a pen out of me!"

Before Yek Ling could say a word, the pencil case had made a dash out of the classroom. Almost everyone in class except the teacher saw a cute little yellow lion with a brown mane making a run out of the classroom on its four stubby feet!

The little lion ran quickly along a corridor, making a rattling sound as it passed a row of classes. All the students in all the classes heard the rattling sound as the little lion ran except the teachers.

A little boy in the first class that the little lion passed could not help but hollered. "Little lion, little lion; Where are you hurrying to?"

The little lion ignored him and was glad when the boy's teacher boxed his ears for hollering.

"Serve you right for being a busybody," the little lion had instead said as it made a face and stuck out a tongue.

A sweet little girl in the next class was luckier. When she asked the little lion where it was going, the latter merely shook its head.

"I haven't given that a thought," the little lion then told another girl in a blue pinafore from another class.

"All I know is that I am not going to stand still and let a silly, proud little boy show off my pens to some strangers," the little lion said.

"I doubt you have any pen at all," a bespectacled boy had then told the lion.

"Of course, I do!" The little lion retorted, slightly annoyed. "I even have some good quality pencils, erasers and a red sharpener and they are all brand new," it said with pride.

"You aren't carrying a bag, are you?" The boy then asked. "Where would you be keeping all these things?"

The little lion then smiled. It seemed extremely pleased as if it had outsmarted the boy.

"See, you'd better believed it if I tell you that you are just a little greenhorn who has yet to see the world," The little lion said. "You don't have to have a bag to carry things, you know."

Bending down and pointing a paw at its back, the little lion had then added, "See the zipper there? If you unzip it, you will find all my pens, pencils, erasers and a red sharpener inside."

The boy unzipped the zipper and did indeed find the pens, pencils, erasers and a red sharper. He quickly scooped them all out and distributed them among his friends. Perhaps, you would feel that this would serve the little lion right, which of course, I agree.

23

An Invisible Boy

Kok Chuan loved to eat. He was always eating and was actually pigging out when his friend, Ah Chin came over to his house to return his comics. He was putting the last spoonful of fried *koay teow* into his already oily mouth and flushing it down his throat with a big mug of hot Milo when Ah Chin said, "At the rate you are eating, you'll get very fat in no time!"

Kok Chuan was already a fat boy. He could not imagine himself getting any fatter.

"How I wish I am an invisible boy," Kok Chuan said. "Then, I can go on eating my favourite food without having to worry about what others think of my body." He still remembered that his family doctor had said he was slightly obese and his school chums had teased him about his burgeoning figure. He was really growing very round like a ball!

Poor Kok Chuan! He just could not control his urge to eat. His stomach had started to growl again immediately after Ah Chin left. He decided to make himself a big bowl of cereal filled with a big helping of Californian raisins. Yummy! Kok Chuan could feel his mouth water!

Kok Chuan skipped quickly over to the kitchen. As he skipped, he felt his body getting unusually light. His body had become so light that he felt as if he was flying to the kitchen.

Kok Chuan took a big blue porcelain bowl and a silver spoon from a shelf. He got some milk from the refrigerator and was about to pour it on the cereal in the bowl when he felt a warm tingling sensation running through his body.

His little finger had then become very itchy too. When he scratched it, the skin immediately peeled off but there was nothing underneath the skin!

Kok Chuan's little finger had disappeared!

Even before Kok Chuan could figure out what had happened, the skin of his little finger vanished! Another of his finger disappeared into nothingness and another and another! His right hand had vanished completely and so had his left hand and his two feet!

Kok Chuan rushed to his room to look at himself in the mirror His face was devoid of blood but instead of getting very pale, it had turned greenish! His hair was standing on ends; his lips, which were purplish, were quivering while his eyeballs were turning red and were rolling uncontrollably!

Kok Chuan felt as if he was exploding! His eyes started seeing stars and then his face became distorted and he saw his image disappeared from the mirror!

Kok Chuan had turned invisible!

Kok Chuan could still see the yellow T-shirt and the navy blue Bermuda shorts he was wearing. They were standing upright on their own, devoid of legs, hands and head! When Kok Chuan took them off, he found his entire body missing! Kok Chuan had indeed turned completely invisible. He had his wish to become invisible fulfilled!

A little elf was sitting on the windowsill when Kok Chuan had made his wish earlier. It had heard Kok Chuan and unknown to Kok Chuan, had granted him his wish!

You'd have thought that Kok Chuan was happy beyond words but far from it! His mother could not see him and was terrified when she heard him called.

And worse still, when Kok Chuan longed for a hug from his mother, he could not get it since his mother could not find him!

You would not want to be an invisible boy now, would you?

24

Orang Utan Island

Hing Chye and Wei Boon were both enjoying themselves swimming in the river. Earlier, Hing Chye had suggested that the boys went for a swim. As it was a terribly hot day, Wei Boon was quick to go along with the idea.

"Let's take a dip over there," Hing Chye had said, pointing his short stubby finger at a cool spot which was under the shade of a big banyan tree.

The boys rushed to the said spot and dived together into the river. Hing Chye and Wei Boon were both having marvellous time splashing water at each other when a log drifted into the scene. The log drifted near Hing Chye who was quick to climb onto it.

"Come on, Wei Boon," Hing Chye said, "Let's take a ride on this log."

Wei Boon immediately climbed up the log to join Hing Chye. The boy paddled the log with their bare hands and before they knew it, they had paddled themselves to a lovely green island.

"What a beautiful island this is!" Hing Chye exclaimed. Both the boys had then jumped down from the log to rush to the shore of the lovely island. They had heard a shout for help coming from some bushes and had run there to investigate. They had thought that another boy was in trouble but imagine their surprise then when they were confronted instead by a terribly upset little *orang utan*, which had got himself entangled in a bush.

As the boys stood there, dumbfounded and their face pale with fright, the *orang utan* said, as if to confirm, "Yes, yes, it was me who had shouted for help just now. An *orang utan* can speak too, you know. After all, this is *Orang Utan Island!*"

"Won't you two come and release me from this mess now?" The *orang utan* then added.

The boys did not just help the little *orang utan* but they did also get very warm with him very quickly. They found it very hard to remain afraid of the extremely friendly and charming animal, which called himself, BJ.

BJ took the boys home to his house, which was a quaint little wooden cottage surrounded by a well-kept garden. There was a big tree with a big nest of twigs on top in the garden. BJ said it was his very own tree house and was proud of the fact that he had built it all by himself.

The little *orang utan* then invited the boys to go indoors to a cosy living room where they sat on a blue settee to watch an *orang utan* football match on television.

When the programme took a break for commercials, Hing Chye looked up and saw a picture of a huge, unfriendly-looking adult *orang utan* on the beige wall.

Almost immediately, the boys heard thundering footsteps outside.

"Fo Fee Fo Fi Fom!" An equally thundering voice boomed. "I smell of sweet little boys in the house!"

"Nicky is back!" BJ then exclaimed excitedly. "You'd better be gone! Nicky dislikes human beings. He thinks *Orang Utan* Island is only for *orang utans*!"

BJ immediately ushered the boys out of the house through the back door.

The boys ran as quickly as their feet could carry them to the river.

Once there, they both dived together into the river. They had to swim home since the log they rode on earlier had disappeared. The boys were glad they were both good swimmers and that they had not met BJ's uncle, Nicky. They dared not think of what Nicky would do to them if he had met them but both were sure that they would not help Nicky if he were the one entangled in the bush.

25

A Different Thought

A kind farmer once made a pilgrimage to a temple on top of a mountain with his wife. The couple had been married for several years and since they were still childless, they had planned to go there to pray for a child.

The farmer's wife woke up very early to prepare for the journey. She packed both of them some food and like a lark, smiled sweetly and chatted gaily as she trudged beside her husband on a weathered beaten path.

Halfway through their journey, the couple came to a swift flowing river. Heavy rains had washed the bridge away the day before and the couple had no choice but to wade across the river.

Upon reaching the other bank, the couple had come face to face with an old lady who had sitting beside her on a rock, her pretty teenage daughter. Both mother and daughter had looked rather sad and forlorn and the farmer could not help but asked, "What troubles you, dear old lady?"

"I have just made a pilgrimage to the temple on top of the mountain to pray for my ailing husband," The old woman replied, "I am hurrying home now to tend to him but alas, the rain had washed away the bridge and I am stranded here. I am just too old to wade across the swift flowing river and my daughter is too young and scared."

Seized by a sudden pity, the farmer without hesitation offered to carry both the old lady and her daughter on his back across the river. He had to make two tiring trips, to and fro, across the river; first to carry the old lady and then, her daughter but he had felt it was all a worthwhile effort.

From this point of the journey onwards, the farmer had however noticed a sudden change of behaviour in his wife. The latter had suddenly turned gloomy and quiet. She uttered hardly a word for the rest of the journey and ate hardly a mouthful when they rested to eat. She had even become pretty moody.

On their return journey, the farmer decided to ask his wife the reason for this sudden transformation.

Upon prodding, she had reluctantly said, "I can't forget the other day when we had to wade across the river. You had let me wade on my own but do not hesitate to carry another lady. Naturally, ideas will creep into my mind and I can't help but feel jealous especially when there is a pretty young lady involved."

The farmer was dumbfounded when he heard his wife spoke thus.

Then, when he found the words, he slowly said, "I think I was only thinking of helping others then."

His wife could not help feeling ashamed when he added quietly, "I don't deny having carried the young pretty girl on my back but do you have to carry her still in your heart?"

26

Drunken Monkeys

Remy and Marty were two of the most adventurous monkeys around. One day, Remy suggested that they go mountain climbing and Marty was quick to jump at the idea. The latter had been bored stiff with just climbing trees and had thought climbing mountain would be a nice change of routine.

The two monkeys then wasted no time in getting ready for their trip. They got out their blue and green knap-sacks respectively and filled them with so much food that one would think that the monkeys were going away for weeks.

Being the good friends they were, both Remy and Marty had actually packed enough food for the both of them and being the mischievous monkeys they were too, both had also planned to play tricks on each other. Unknown to each other, both had emptied each other's knapsack and filled it with little pebbles and stones instead.

Imagine the two poor monkeys huffing and puffing up the trail up the mountain! Both were grinning from ear to ear at each other, feeling very pleased, thinking that the

85

other had sweated as a result of the heavy load of pebbles and stones in the knapsacks. Both of course, were unaware that each had himself sweated because of the same uncalled for heavy load.

It was not surprising then that very soon; the two monkeys were almost out of their breath and were panting heavily for water.

Remy suggested that the two of them stop to rest.

Marty again jumped at Remy's suggestion.

The two monkeys were also getting very hungry and decided then to have their lunch. They picked a spot under a shady tree. Each pretended to unpack the knapsacks slowly as they waited in anticipation of the other crying out in surprise.

Imagine next the scene when the two monkeys jumped and cried simultaneously in surprise! Both were extremely shocked to find their knapsacks filled almost to the brim with pebbles and stones. They were also both very hungry and thirsty but there was neither a bite to eat nor a drop to drink!

One would think then that Remy and Marty would jump at each other's throat but they knew better. They were both at fault for playing a silly trick on each other.

Remy could only suggest that the two of them turn back and make for home.

Marty however, thought they were already too far away in their journey. Besides, Marty was really very, very tired and he would not take another step even if a horse were to drag him.

Both Remy and Marty needed to drink and eat to replenish their energy and were the two monkeys in luck indeed!

A big red juicy fruit had fallen with a plod on Remy's head. Suddenly, the two monkeys realized they were resting under a tree laden with big red juicy fruits!

Remy found the fruit to be deliciously sweet sour.

Both monkeys decided to make a feast of them. The two monkeys ate as many fruits as they could. They ate until their bellies bulged like a fully blown balloon. Then, their heads started to throb uncontrollably.

Remy began to sway his hips while Marty's tail twitched as it took on a life of its own.

Both monkeys then rolled on the ground, only to get up again to gyrate to the rhythm of the sound of the leaves rustling in the wind.

A deer and a doe passed by just then and glared with disdain at Remy and Marty.

"Just look at those two drunken monkeys!" The doe said.

The deer spat at the monkeys and said, "Only greedy and foolish animals would spoil their health by getting so dead drunk!"

It seemed that Remy and Marty had got themselves drunk by eating the fruits, which had fermented and had a high content of alcohol.

It would be important to watch what you eat, don't you think?

27

Dragon Seed

Yew Jin was covered with dirt from head to toe! He had had just a rough game of football with his buddies.

"Do go and get a bath immediately," Yew Jin's mother reprimanded.

Yew Jin had a long bath but when he emerged from the bathroom, his mother said, "You did not wash behind your ears! There is enough dirt there for a seed to grow!

Yew Jin ignored his mother and that night when he was sound asleep, a little green dragon crept up to his ear and planted a magic seed there!

Yew Jin woke up the next morning feeling very refreshed. When he went to the bathroom to brush his teeth, he looked into the mirror and boy! Was he surprised indeed to see something greenish behind his right ear! He examined his ear and found a little seedling growing there! He was amazed to see the stem of the seedling growing rapidly. It crept up his right temple, grew across his forehead and almost encircled his entire head!

"Ah! It looks like I am wearing a green headband! That's cool! I do look like a tennis player!" Yew Jin exclaimed and flexed his biceps. He swung his hands and pretended he hit a tennis ball with an imaginary tennis racket.

As he was practising his strokes, a leaf grew upright. It looks like a little green feather on his head!

"There is a little seedling growing behind my ear and its leaf is growing so long that it makes me look like a little Red Indian boy with a feather on his head!" Yew Jin said excitedly. He was so pleased with the plant behind his ear that he decided to leave it there.

Just as Yew Jin finished talking, young shoots began to sprout from the stem of the seedling. The green headband on Yew Jin's head had begun to look like a crown of leaves!

Yew Jin took a white towel and spread it across his chest. He let the towel hang on his shoulder and it made him look like he was wearing a toga.

"I think I do look like someone learned from the Roman Empire!" Yew Jin said.

He started marching out of the bathroom with his nose up in the air, pretending that he was someone important.

When Yew Jin next turned back to look into the mirror, the green crown on his head had grown into an untidy green mess! Now, Yew Jin seemed more like wearing a green helmet!

"Hmm…" Yew Jin thought, "This would camouflage me very well if I am in the jungle, hiding in some bushes from my enemies."

Yew Jin pretended to be a soldier. He aimed a finger at his image in the mirror and pretended to shoot it with this make belief rifle.

"How nice it would be if a little bird builds a nest on my head!" Yew Jin then thought. He could picture a little yellow bird fetching twigs to build a nest on his head. The little yellow bird would lay and hatch its eggs there and each morning, Yew Jin would be able to watch it feed its nestlings!

"How nice indeed if a little bird does make its home here! At least then, I could get to hear it sing each morning," Yew Jin muttered dreamily.

Little flower buds had however, begun to appear on the now fully grown plant on Yew Jin's head. There were flower buds all over Yew Jin's head and they were beginning to blossom!

In no time at all, Yew Jin's head was covered with bright red flowers which emitted a pleasant smell. The flowers attracted a swarm of bees that happened to be flying past Yew Jin's house.

Poor Yew Jin! Could you imagine him running all over town with a plant full of blooming flowers on his head? He did just that to get away from the bees!

For just having dirt behind the ears, you'd probably have thought that was a high price to pay!

28

A Car For Poh Choan

Poh Choan was late! He dashed across the road to Wah Cheong's house but the latter had already left! Poh Choan would not be able to attend their friend's birthday party!

Poh Choan had earlier made a pact with Wah Cheong. He was to meet Wah Cheong in the latter's house at about half past six and the latter's father would drive both of them to town to attend their friend's birthday party.

Poh Choan had however, been half an hour late and Wah Cheong had left without him. Perhaps, he deserved to miss his only means of transport to town. He had spent the whole afternoon in a neighbour's house, chatting and had forgotten the time!

When Poh Choan was walking home, he bumped head on into a plump woman in a long, flowing purple gown.

Seeing him so crest-fallen, the woman with the round, kindly face had asked, "What's troubling you, dear child?"

Poh Choan unhesitant, told her of his predicament.

The woman offered her help at once. "I can fix your problem easily," she said confidently.

Flashing a smile, the woman had then produced a thin silver stick from under her broad sleeves. The silver stick had at one end, a little twinkling silver star which emitted bright blue sparks! It looked like a magic wand and the woman who suddenly, spotted a glowing yellow halo round her head, undoubtedly was a fairy!

"I am your fairy God-aunt!" The woman had then said as if to confirm. She waved her wand and suddenly, a golden pumpkin-shaped carriage drawn by six white horses with pink feathers on their heads, appeared before PohChoan's very surprised eyes.

"I can't ride that to town!" Poh Choan could not help but exclaimed. "Nobody travels in a horse-drawn carriage anymore. I'll be the laughing stock," he said.

The fairy was rather understanding and obliging.

She gave another wave of her wand and the carriage immediately disappeared. In its place was a bicycle! The bicycle had a rather small front wheel and one very big back wheel!

"What a funny bicycle! I bet I can't balance myself on that!" Poh Choan said of the penny-farthing. "Besides, a bicycle just won't do. The town is just too far and riding a bicycle would be just too tiring."

Then, before the fairy could make another wave of her wand, Poh Choan had added, "Don't give me a motorcycle either. I am too young and do not have licence to ride one."

"Give me a car. Yes! A big flashy car with a chauffeur would do just great!" Poh Choan finally said, his big round eyes, gleaming!

And so that was it!

Poh Choan got a big flashy Cadillac with tinted windows. The car had even a bunch of decorative flowers on the bonnet and a thin man with a ratty face for a chauffeur.

The chauffeur was smartly dressed in a black tuxedo.

When he opened the door for Poh Choan, the latter was surprised to find a bridegroom and a bride sitting at the back of the car. He turned to look at his benefactor, who merely shrugged her shoulder and explained, "That's the best I could do. That's the only car available at the moment. You'll have to share it with the poor couple who had also wished for a car. I couldn't turn down the poor couple who had prayed fervently for a Cadillac to ferry them to their wedding luncheon, could I?"

So, in this way, Poh Choan got to attend his friend's birthday party.

Later, when it was time to go home, he chose to return with Wah Cheong.

The Cadillac was waiting for him then but he felt more comfortable in the company of his friend, Wah Cheong. He did not mind at all riding in an old dilapidated car.

29

A Mid-autumn Festival

The mid-autumn festival had come again! Chee Keong could not contain his joy! His father had bought him a beautiful traditional lantern in the shape of a Chinese dragon. His mother had bought him enough candles to last a month! How lucky he was!

Chee Keong had always looked forward to the mid-autumn festival which falls each year on the eight month of the Chinese lunar calendar. Chinese children all the world over would celebrate by carrying lanterns of various shapes, sizes and hues for days before the festival climaxes on the fifteen day of the month.

Chee Keong had looked forward to the festival mainly because it gave him the opportunity to gather with his friends from the neighbourhood. In the little town where he lived, the pace of life was not just slow but it would come almost to a standstill at night. The lantern festival brought some life and colour to the little town when each night, almost all the children there were allowed by their parents to stroll the streets until very late into the night. Together, they would light up their sleepy little town with their beautiful lanterns and turned it into a fairyland. How beautiful and colourful the scene was then! And how enjoyable the whole affair was!

One night, Chee Keong and his friends strolled to the outskirt of town. Normally, they would just take their lanterns around town and would then stop at the gates of their school where they would sit and chat before turning back for home.

"Let's walk further tonight!" Chee Keong had suggested. Let's venture further to a place where there is no house and the only light that illuminates the place would be the lights from our lanterns!"

The children did just that and what did they find there? The place was not just pitch dark and deserted. From the lights of their lanterns, they could see the faint outline of an old tree across the road.

The grand old tree by the road had been blown down by the wind and it had fallen across it, threatening to block any vehicle from passing, and worse still, someone may even drive straight into the tree and get himself injured or killed!

Chee Keong and his friends decided to do something about it.

"We can't just drag the tree to the side of the road," Someone said, "The tree is just too big and we are not so strong."

"Maybe, we should just go back to town and get some help," Someone else said.

They however, did not have to wait long to decide.

There was a loud screeching sound like a brake being stepped on and a car suddenly came to a halt in front of them.

An elderly man on a business trip had returned home. Driving very fast, he would have driven straight into the fallen tree had he not been alerted from afar.

Earlier in his car, the man had dreamily listened to the pop song that was playing from his cassette recorder. Then, suddenly, he saw lights in the distance.

A big group of children holding lanterns of various shapes, sizes and hues was standing before him. Behind them, he could see the outline of the fallen tree.

There is much to rejoice when a man's life is saved!

30

Hats off!

Han Beng and his friends had made a pact to wake up early on Sunday morning. They had made an appointment to meet at the foot of a beautiful green hill at half past six. The boys had planned to climb the hill together. They were naturally very excited since that was something they had not done for ages.

All of Han Beng's friends were early for their appointment. Han Beng however, had come ten minutes late, looking pretty drowsy and he was wearing a big straw hat too!

"Why are you wearing such a funny straw hat? Eng Lai could not help asking.

"It would not be noon for a very long while yet and you won't expect the sun to be very hot until then," Swee Lim said.

"Your hat is too big for you," Kok Lam then said, "You look like one of those Mexicans in an old cowboy movie!"

Han Beng was puzzled as he felt his head with his hands. "Did I put on a hat?" He asked, surprised. "I can't remember putting anything on my head," he said.

He took his hat off but after glancing at it and fiddling its broad brim, had promptly put it on.

"I do look good in this hat, don't you think?" He asked as he adjusted the hat on his head. "Besides looking like a character from an old western, I think the hat is rather useful. It can keep my head warm and cosy in this chilly weather," he added with a laugh.

The hat had in fact, also kept Han Beng dry.

There was a slight drizzle when the boys trekked up a weather-beaten track up the hill. All the boys except Han Beng, were wet when they reached the peak.

The breeze had then blown Han Beng's hat off his head and suddenly it was floating in the air like a kite minus its strings.

Han Beng tried to catch hold of his hat but it had flown too far and too high. When it floated near Swee Lim, the latter jumped to catch it. He managed to catch hold of it but just when he was returning it to its owner, the hat had been blown off his hand.

The hat flew up in the air, hanging there above the boys momentarily as if teasing them. Then, when it floated down again, both Eng Lai and Kok Lam ran after it. They failed to retrieve the hat but had instead, knocked against each other!

The hat then flew up and down, swirled round and round and all the boys were sent scurrying here and there as they tried to catch hold of it. No one, however, succeeded in his endeavour. Han Beng and Swee Lim came close to touching the hat but each time, the breeze would blow the hat out of their reach. The boys had however, enjoyed themselves chasing the hat.

"That was a great one!" All the boys had said simultaneously when the breeze finally subsided and the hat came to rest on the ground just in front of Han Beng.

The boys were by then, huffing and puffing away and were pretty hot from all the running.

Han Beng picked up the hat and fanned himself with it.

"This is really a very useful hat." He said and added, "I hope my grandmother won't miss it when she does her gardening today!"

Stories
To Celebrate Life

Eng Foo Tiam, a teacher by profession, spends his entire life teaching young boys and girls. 'Stories to celebrate life' has been written with his students in mind, especially those who inspire him, whom he loves and who have become his lifelong friends. 'Stories to celebrate life' celebrates some of their moments together.

'Stories to Celebrate Life' contains 30 very short stories such as 'Celebration of Life', 'The Seventh Step', 'Orang Utan Island', 'Rainbow in Her Heart' and many other stories which most of the time transport you out of this mundane world into a world of fantasy where animals and inanimate objects act and talk like human beings as each live through a moment in time just as human beings live through each moment of theirs. Told simply and quickly, the old fashion and not so old fashion stories tease the idle mind. Some may tug at your heartstrings and others may leave you chuckling and wanting for more. When there is a touch of Zen, it will leave you wondering about life itself…

PARTRIDGE
A Penguin Random House Company

ISBN 978-1-4828-2886-3

90000

9 781482 828863